To Eric and Vickie whose unconditional love continuously
has a profound impact on my life. I love you.

Acknowledgements:
I'd like to thank my editor, Victoria Rock, for her unwavering support for me and this book;
Karen Pike for her excellent taste; Kendra Marcus for her clarity and wisdom; and my parents
for teaching me through their example that a vision is achievable.

Library of Congress Cataloging-in-Publication Data
Hubbard. Woodleigh.
  C is for curious / Woodleigh Hubbard.
     p.   cm.
  Summary: Presents an alphabet of emotions, from angry to zealous.
  ISBN 0-87701-679-8
  1. Emotions—Juvenile literature. 2. Alphabet—Juvenile literature. [1. Emotions. 2. Alphabet.] I. Title.
BF561.H82   1990
152.4—dc20
[E]
                                                                                    90-1770
                                                                                       CIP
                                                                                        AC

10 9 8 7 6 5 4 3 2

Chronicle Books
275 Fifth Street
San Francisco, California 94103

C IS FOR CURIOUS

AN
A B C
O F
F E E L I N G S

BY
WOODLEIGH
HUBBARD

CHRONICLE BOOKS · SAN FRANCISCO

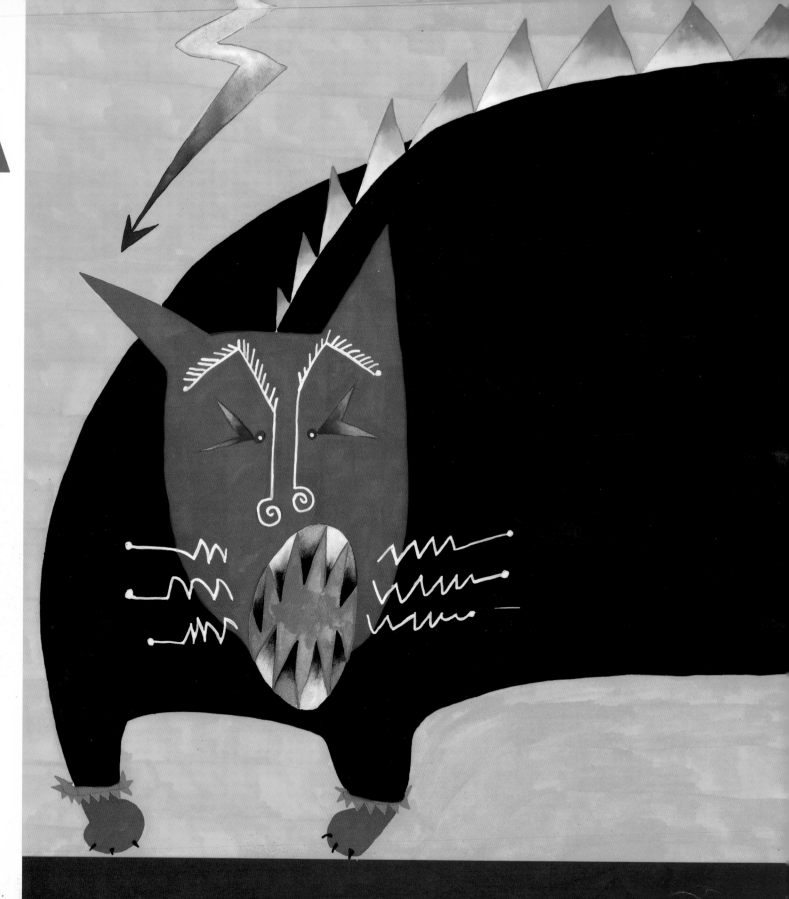

ANGRY

BORED

CURIOUS

DOUBTFUL

FRIGHTENED

GIGGLY

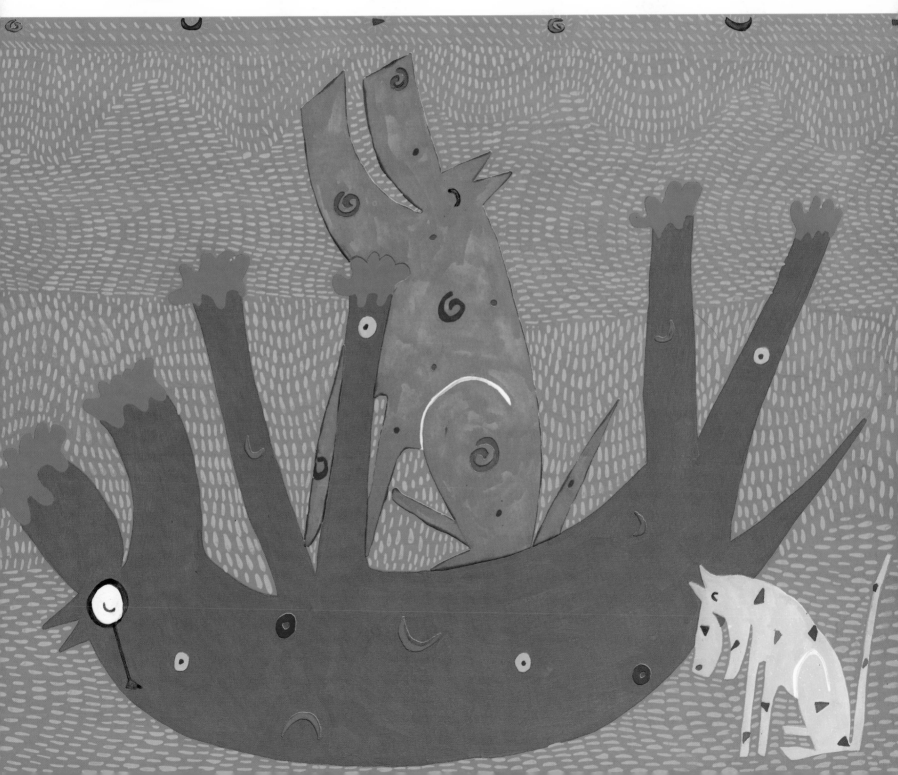

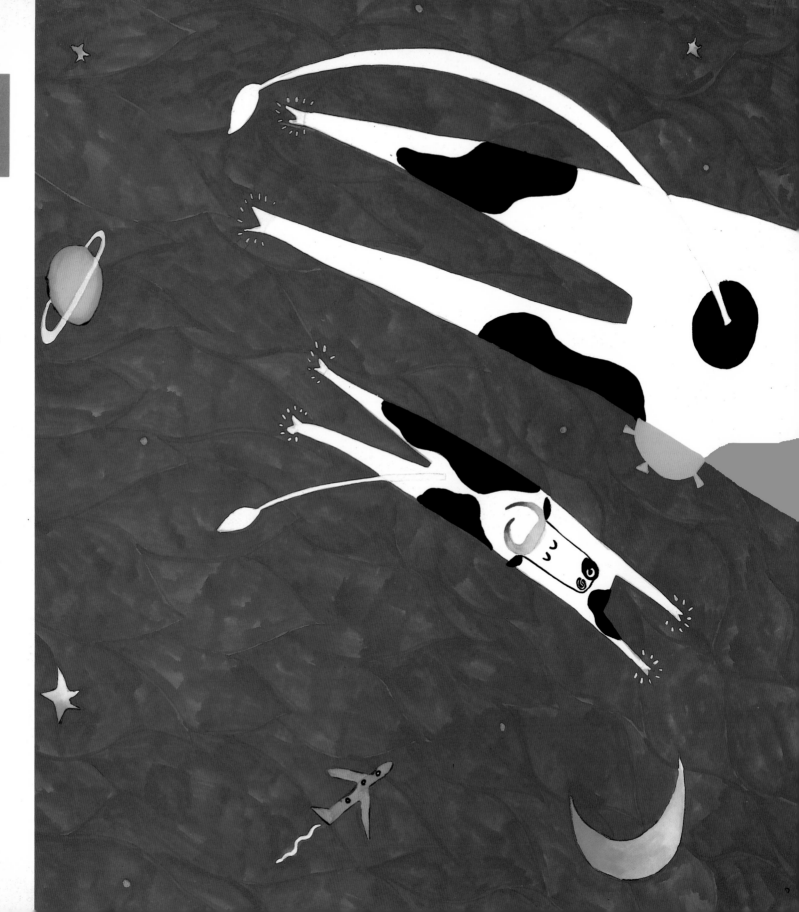

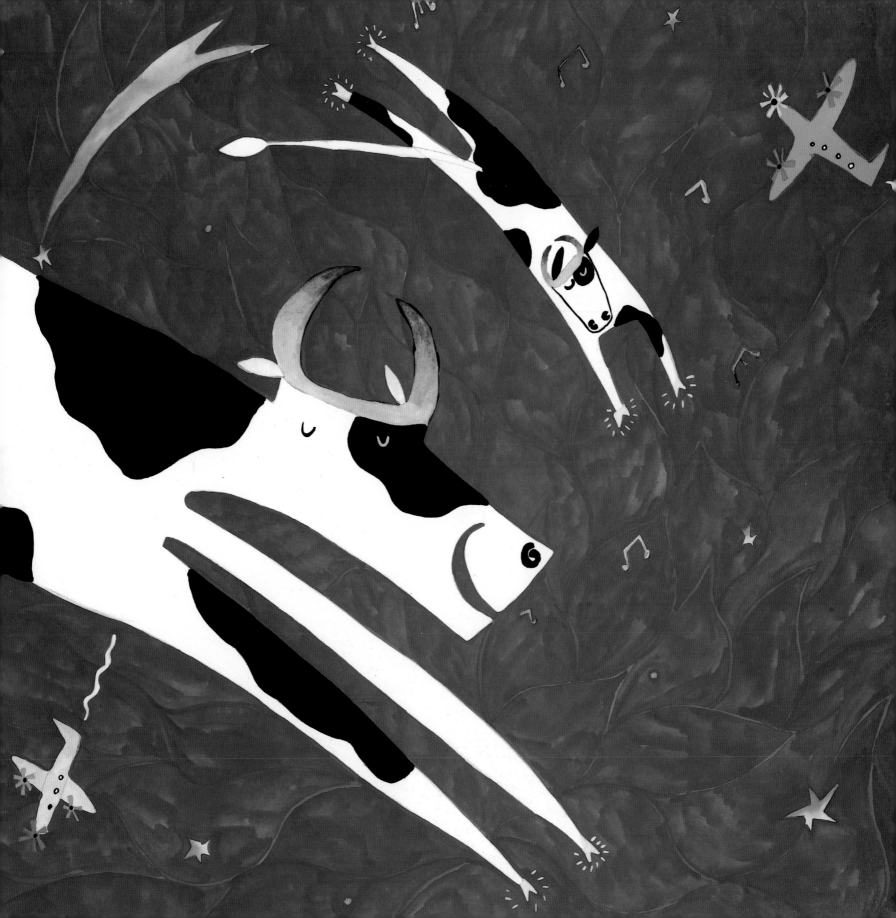

IMPATIENT

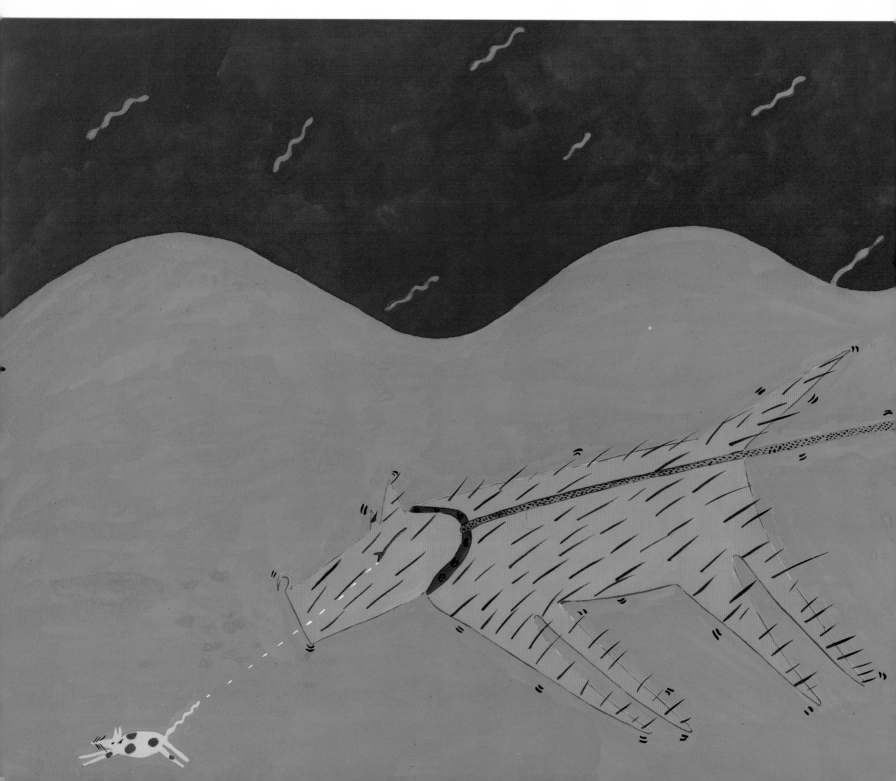

JEALOUS

KIND

LOVING

MOODY

OBEDIENT

PLAYFULL

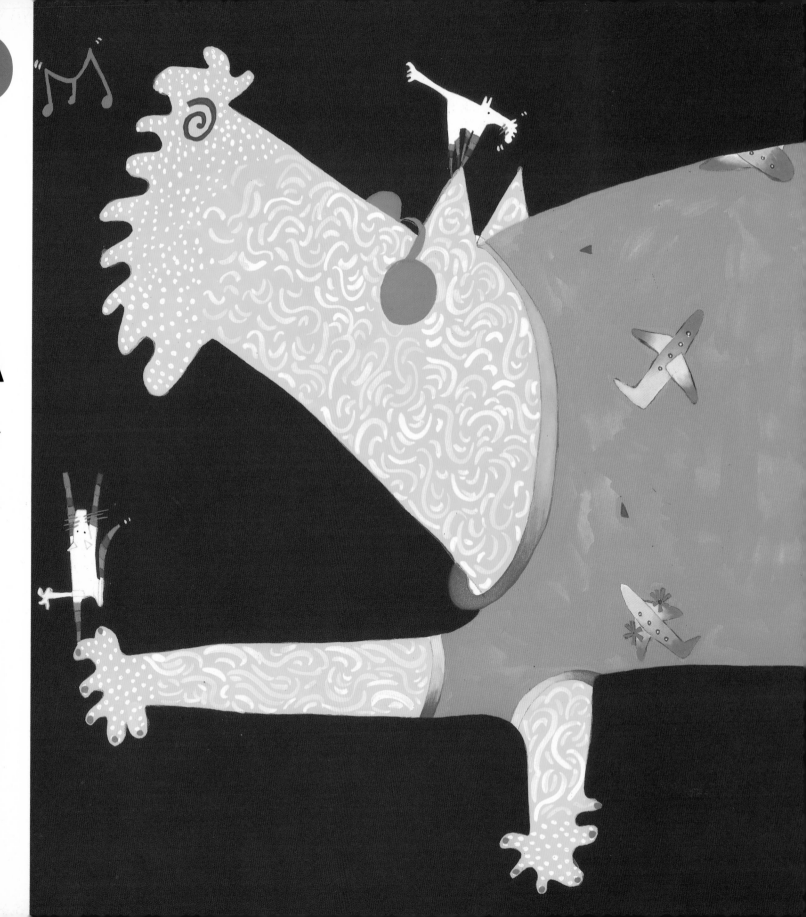

QUIET

RESTLESS

S
H
Y

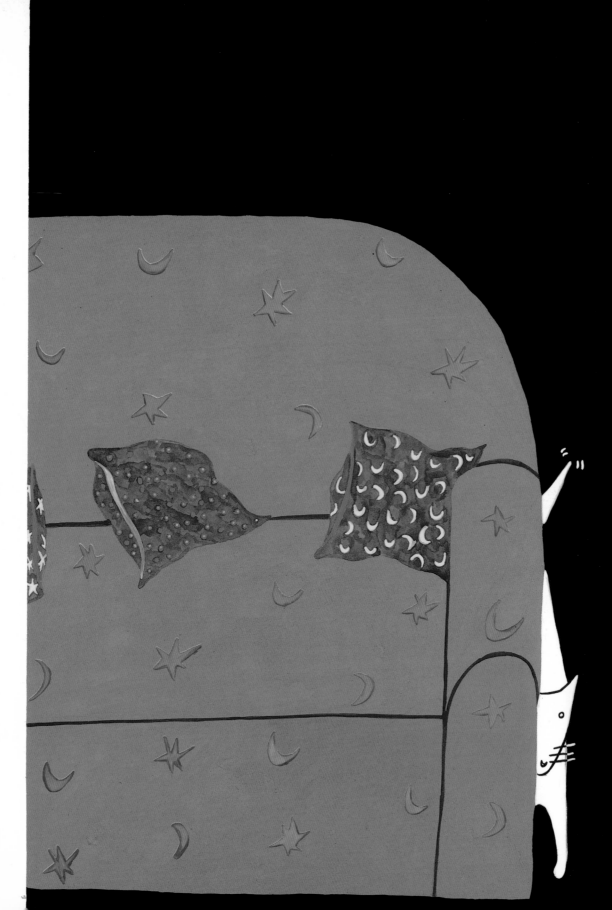

TEARFUL

UNDER

STANDING

V A I N

me me me me me me me me
me me me me me me me me
me me me me me me me me
me me me me me me me
me me me me me me me
me me me me me me me
me me me me me me me

WILD

Xenophobic

YUCKY

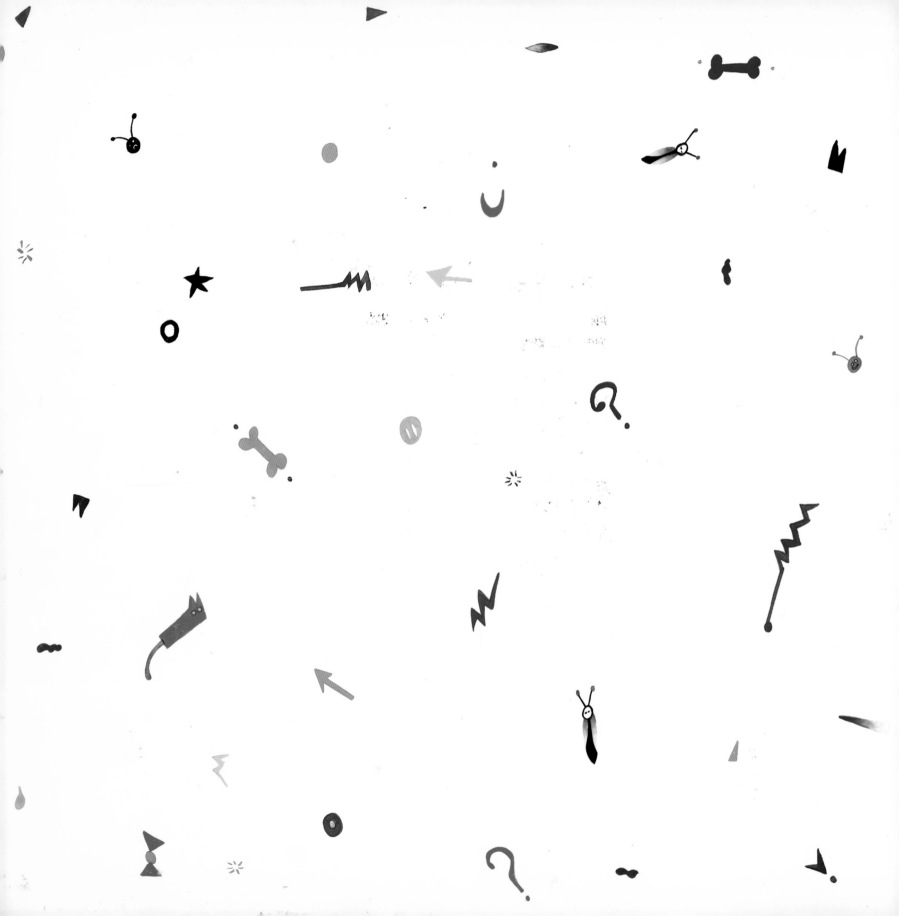